How Mama Brought the Spring

Fran Manushkin

Illustrated by **Holly Berry**

DUTTON CHILDREN'S BOOKS

For grandma Beatrice's great-grandson,
Michael Alan Buzil
—F.M.

For my daughters,
Isobel and Gwendolyn
—H.B.

DUTTON CHILDREN'S BOOKS
A division of Penguin Young Readers Group

Published by the Penguin Group
Penguin Group (USA) Inc., 375 Hudson Street, New York, New York 10014, U.S.A.
Penguin Group (Canada), 90 Eglinton Avenue East, Suite 700, Toronto, Ontario, Canada M4P 2Y3
(a division of Pearson Penguin Canada Inc.)
Penguin Books Ltd, 80 Strand, London WC2R 0RL, England
Penguin Ireland, 25 St Stephen's Green, Dublin 2, Ireland (a division of Penguin Books Ltd)
Penguin Group (Australia), 250 Camberwell Road, Camberwell, Victoria 3124, Australia
(a division of Pearson Australia Group Pty Ltd)
Penguin Books India Pvt Ltd, 11 Community Centre, Panchsheel Park, New Delhi - 110 017, India
Penguin Group (NZ), 67 Apollo Drive, Rosedale, North Shore 0632, New Zealand
(a division of Pearson New Zealand Ltd)
Penguin Books (South Africa) (Pty) Ltd, 24 Sturdee Avenue, Rosebank, Johannesburg 2196, South Africa
Penguin Books Ltd, Registered Offices: 80 Strand, London WC2R 0RL, England

CIP Data is available.

Published in the United States by Dutton Children's Books,
a division of Penguin Young Readers Group
345 Hudson Street, New York, New York 10014
www.penguin.com/youngreaders

Designed by Sara Reynolds and Abby Kuperstock

Manufactured in China • First Edition
ISBN 978-0-525-42027-9
10 9 8 7 6 5 4 3 2 1

"ROSY LEVINE, will you *please* get up?" called her mother.

"I'm trying," Rosy groaned. It's true, Rosy *did* try. She opened her eyes and looked outside. But what was there to see? The same gray Chicago sky and more soggy snow. And where was the sun? It hadn't shown its face for weeks.

So when Rosy's mother called again from the kitchen, "Rosy, are you *ever* getting up?" Rosy hugged her cat, Moishe, and they both closed their eyes again.

"Rosy!" Now her mother was next to her bed. "Get up!" she said.

"No!" Rosy grumped. "I'm sick of winter. I want spring."

"Who doesn't?" agreed Mrs. Levine. "I want spring so badly, I can almost taste it. Sit up and drink some juice, and I'll tell you a story about Minsk."

Rosy smiled and opened her eyes. She loved her mother's stories about when she was a girl in Minsk, in Belarus, a country near Russia.

Mrs. Levine began: "I'm going to tell you how your Grandma
Beatrice brought spring to Minsk."

Rosy giggled.

"You don't believe me? I was there! Listen closely—
I won't leave out a thing."

First I'll tell you about our winters in Minsk. Winters today—
what *are* they? A few little puffs and they're done. But years ago,
those young Siberian winds could hold their breath for hundreds of
miles. And then—*whoosh!*—they'd swoop down on Minsk!

The snowdrifts grew higher and higher—touching the sky. Day after day, month after month, my mama and papa and I lived in a shivery kingdom of snow. Well, one morning, Rosy, just like you, I'd had enough. "Mama!" I shouted. "I'm sick of winter! I'm not getting up until spring!"

"Is that so?" she told me. "I didn't know my daughter was a bear."

"I am," I growled, and I burrowed deeper into my goose-down cave.

"Suit yourself," Mama said. So I did, reading my book by the snowy light.

But in a little while, I heard Mama beginning to sing: "*Di-deedle-dee! Di-deedle-deedle-dee.*"

Right away, I had to poke my head out, because whenever Mama sang, she was up to something.

"*Di-deedle-dee. Di-deedle-deedle-dee.*" And then she started to hum.

Oh, I just had to know, so I threw back my covers and tiptoed, shivering, toward her song.

"Put on your slippers!" Mama told me without turning around. That's how *smart* mamas were back then!

So I did, and then I padded back to Mama. She was all wrapped up in sweaters and shawls, and she had coiled her braids and placed them on her neck like a little warm rug.

Crack-crack! Mama was breaking eggs into a bowl. Then she stirred in flour and some milk too.

"What are you making?" I asked.

"It's not a snowman," Mama teased. And she made up
this song while she stirred:

"When I save enough eggs,
I run out of milk.
If there's money for cheese,
I have none for flour.
And sugar! Sugar is rarer than silk.
But look! Today I have them all:
eggs and milk, flour and cheese and sugar—
all at the same time."

"Here," Mama instructed. "Unfold this cloth and put it on the
table."
I unfolded the blue cloth and spread it out nice and smooth.
Mama gave her batter one last stir.

Then she poured a little batter into a pan on the fire, swirling it around until it coated the bottom.

Soon it was sizzling, and when the edges curled up, Mama said, "Watch!" And she flipped out a perfect circle.

"What is it?" I asked. Mama still wouldn't tell. But whatever she was doing, I wanted to do it too.

"Of course you can." Mama nodded. "As soon as you go get dressed."

"Oh, Mama!" I groaned. But did I have any choice? I changed from my sleeping to my waking clothes and rushed right back.

"Here!" Mama handed me the bowl. "Pour some batter into the pan and swirl it around. Wait for it to sizzle a little—then flip it onto the tablecloth."

Well, that was hard to remember, but I did.

Pour, swirl, sizzle, FLIP!
Pour, swirl, sizzle, FLIP!
Pour, swirl, sizzle, FLIP!

One by one, I lined up golden circles on the tablecloth,
like sunflowers against a blue sky.

Between the eighth and ninth sunflower, Papa came in from shoveling snow. "Ah!" He sniffed and smiled at Mama. "I've been waiting for this all winter."

"But what *is* it?" I asked.

"Be patient!" Mama answered. "Do you want me to spoil the surprise?"

Well, of course I didn't.

Now Mama was putting soft cheese, a few eggs, and sugar into a pink bowl. She handed me a fork, saying, "Stir this for me with your strong young arms."

So I stirred and stirred until I felt my stomach stir too.

"I'll take over now," Mama said. "This is the hard part."

As we watched over Mama's shoulder, she dipped her spoon over and over into the pink bowl, and in the middle of each sunny circle she built a little white hill.

"Keep your eyes on Mama's magic hands," Papa said, and believe me I did, as she folded, then rolled those circles up.

Now they were golden and plump!

"What *are* they?" I shouted. I was wild to know.

"Please, a little more patience," urged Mama.

As Mama made row after row of those plump, secret bundles, I felt our house get warmer—and *warmer*. Mama and I shrugged off our shawls, and our braids came loose, tumbling down our backs. Papa's cheeks glowed. "This is my favorite part," he whispered. Mama scooped up three golden bundles and put them in the frying pan. Soon they sizzled so, I saw the ice on our windows melt!

"Papa, give me three plates," Mama said. Then she placed a warm bundle in the middle of each.

I picked up my fork.

"Wait!" Mama spooned on cherry jam, red as flame. "Now!" She beamed. "Let us eat in good health."

I lowered my fork deep into the center of Mama's surprise. Steam swirled as I brought it up to my mouth. I tasted: the gold bundle was warm and smooth and cherry-sweet all at the same time.

"Mama, it's wonderful," I said. "But what *is* it?"

"It's a *blintz!*" Mama announced, looking proud.

"A blintz?" I smiled. "What a perfect name! It tastes just like it sounds—surprising and sweet."

Oh, we three ate like bears after waking from their naps!

And the more we ate, the warmer we were. Papa and I threw off our heavy sweaters, and Mama took off three pairs of socks.

"Look!" Papa pointed. Outside our window, the sun was waking up, too, and melting the snow off the trees. I heard the ice cracking in the stream, and the water began singing a bubbly song.

"Look!" Papa beamed. "Your mama brought spring to Minsk!"

"With blintzes!" I yelled.

Mama nodded modestly, waving her fork around, taming that Siberian wind into a soft, sweet breeze.

"AND SO," said Rosy's mother, finishing her story, "now you know how Grandma Beatrice brought spring to Minsk. The *whole* story— not a word left out!"

"I loved it!" Rosy said. "Look at Moishe!" Her orange kitten was sleeping all bunched up, looking like a little blintz.

"Don't move," Rosy's mother told her. "I want to show you something." She hurried away, humming, and returned cradling something rumply and blue.

"Grandma's blintz tablecloth!" Rosy took hold of one side, and her mother the other, and they unfolded it together.

"Mama," urged Rosy, "let's make blintzes right now. Maybe we can bring spring to Chicago."

"Maybe so!" Her mother nodded. "With blintzes, you never know what can happen!"

Then Rosy and her mother sang:

"We have the eggs and the milk and the cheese,
and the flour and sugar—all at the same time!"

And they went into the kitchen to begin.

Mama's Cheese Blintzes

Wrapper
4 eggs, beaten
1⅓ cup of milk
1 cup of flour
2 tablespoons sugar
Butter, for frying

Filling
2 eggs, beaten
4 teaspoons butter, melted
2 7½ ounce packages
   of farmer cheese
4 tablespoons sugar
½ teaspoon salt
Optional: a pinch of cinnamon

Topping
Jam, to taste
Sour cream, to taste

Preparing the wrapper

■ Combine the eggs and milk in a bowl. Stir in flour and sugar. Beat together until smooth.
■ Melt butter in a small frying pan (nonstick works best!), over medium heat.
■ Drop about 3 tablespoons of batter into the center of the frying pan. Swirl the batter so that it covers the whole bottom of the pan.
■ Cook until small air bubbles form on the top of the wrapper and the bottom is golden brown. Do not turn it over.
■ Using a spatula, flip the wrapper, brown-side up, onto a tablecloth or paper towels.
■ Repeat until all the batter is used up.

Preparing the filling

■ Combine the eggs and butter in a bowl. Add the farmer cheese, sugar, and salt. Mix together well.

Making the blintz

■ With the wrappers brown-side up, place about 3 tablespoons of filling into the center of each one. Repeat until all the filling is used up.
■ Fold the wrapper toward the middle, from opposite sides, covering the filling. Roll up the blintz from the bottom.
■ Fry the blintzes, seam-side down, turning them once to brown both sides.
■ Serve with sour cream or jam. Eat in good health!

Makes about 10 blintzes